W9-CBT-901

Contents

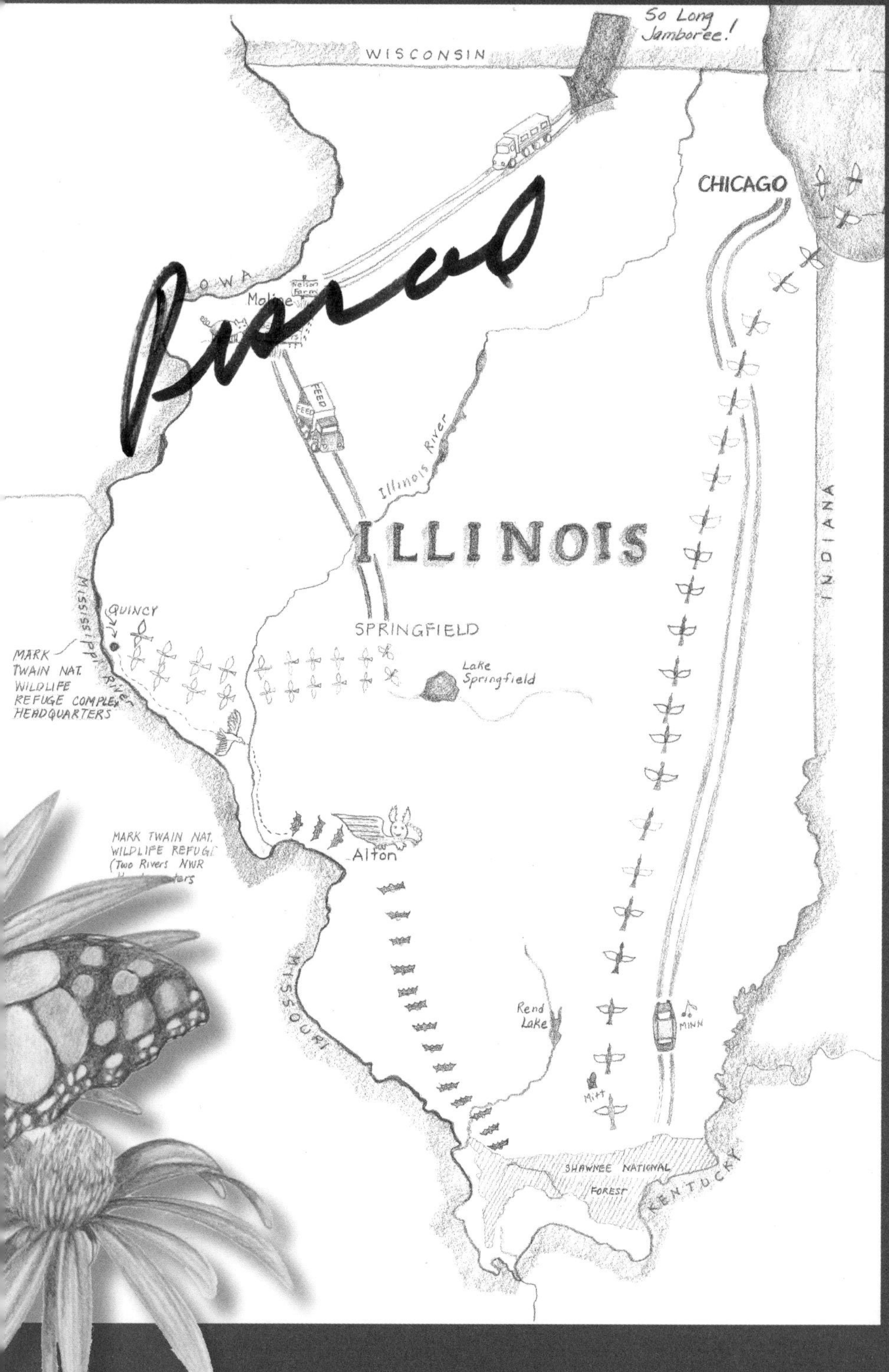
So Long Jamboree!
WISCONSIN
Nelson Farm
Moline
FEED
CHICAGO
Illinois River
ILLINOIS
INDIANA
MISSISSIPPI River
QUINCY
MARK TWAIN NAT. WILDLIFE REFUGE COMPLEX HEADQUARTERS
SPRINGFIELD
Lake Springfield
MARK TWAIN NAT. WILDLIFE REFUGE (Two Rivers NWR
Alton
MISSOURI
Rend Lake
MINN
Mitt
SHAWNEE NATIONAL FOREST
KENTUCKY

Mitt & Minn's Illinois Adventure

by
Kathy-jo Wargin

illustrated by
Karen Busch Holman

All inquiries should be addressed to:
Mitten Press
An imprint of Ann Arbor Media Group LLC
2500 S. State Street
Ann Arbor, MI 48104

Printed and bound by Edwards Brothers, Ann Arbor, Michigan, USA.

10   9   8   7   6   5   4   3   2

Library of Congress Cataloging-in-Publication Data

Wargin, Kathy-jo.
Mitt & Minn's Illinois adventure
by Kathy-jo Wargin ; illustrated by Karen Busch Holman.
p. cm.
Summary: Brother and sister white-footed mice experience exciting
and scary adventures as they desperately search the Midwest for
their parents, who they think are in Chicago, Illinois.
ISBN-13: 978-1-58726-306-4 (hardcover : alk. paper)
ISBN-10: 1-58726-306-8 (hardcover : alk. paper)
[1. Adventure and adventurers--Fiction. 2. White-footed mouse--Fiction.
3. Mice--Fiction. 4. Animals--Fiction. 5. Brothers and sisters--Fiction.
6. Middle West--Fiction.] I. Busch Holman, Karen, 1960- ill.
II. Title. III. Title: Mitt and Minn's Illinois adventure.
PZ7.W234Mis 2007
[Fic]--dc22
2007028854

Book design by Somberg Design
www.sombergdesign.com

CHAPTER ONE

Farewell Jamboree

It was early evening and the last visitor
had left the Wisconsin Cheese Jamboree.
The grounds were empty with the excep-
tion of one dairy farmer busily preparing
his truck for the ride home to Illinois.

Mitt and Minn were excited about the news that Lilka the Jersey cow had shared with them hours earlier. Lilka was from an Illinois farm, but had been at the Jamboree because she and five other Jersey cows had been entered into the dairy cow contest. When Lilka got to know Mitt and Minn, she realized that the pair of mice had parents living in Illinois, on a farm not

far from hers. She told them how their parents had arrived cold, wet, and tired, and that a mouse named Viktor had helped them find a home nearby. Lilka promised Mitt and Minn that if they rode home on the truck with her, she would introduce them to Viktor and Viktor could tell them where their parents were living.

"Mitt," said Minn, "do you think we will make it all the way to Illinois with Lilka? Do you think our parents are really there?"

Mitt was thoughtful before answering his sister. It was only hours earlier that the pair had learned other exciting news—that they were brother and sister. It had been a long day at the Cheese Jamboree, and Mitt thought it seemed like only yesterday that he was living in a mitten in the Mackinaw State Forest of Michigan. When his mitten was stolen, he had no choice but to find it. The journey had taken him through places and dangers he never could have imagined. Now, nestled snug in a barn in Wisconsin with his long-lost sister, he was getting ready to leave for Illinois to be reunited with their parents.

When he spoke, he said matter-of-factly, "Yes, Minn, I think we have both been through enough trials and dangers to get this far. Once we get to Lilka's farm, no matter what, we will find our parents. I do believe the hard part is over."

At that moment, Mitt, the brave white-footed mouse from Michigan, had no idea just how wrong he would be.

CHAPTER TWO

Lilka's Farm

The Jersey cows were asleep in their stalls,
soothed by the drone of the truck engine
purring outside. The
farmer was ready to leave
now, and so he walked
into the barn to
begin loading the
cows one-by-one.
Mitt and Minn
scrambled into
the truck when
it was Lilka's
turn to enter.

Once inside, they climbed on top of her back and rested there while the truck hummed along the freeway. It traveled through the quietest hours of night, leaving Wisconsin and heading over the border into Illinois. Minn and Lilka were tired, and so they slept soundly while the truck hummed along. Mitt was tired too but he could not sleep. He decided not to look out the rear window but, instead, chose to look through the side window so he could think about where he was going, and not where he had been.

When they arrived at the farm, it was as lovely as Lilka had described. There were long white barns surrounded by rows of red geraniums and pretty Shasta daisies. There were straight white fences that made very square corners and a house with large windows and a bright red double door. The farm was outside of Moline, and there was a large painted sign above the barn door that read "Nelson Farm, established 1862."

Mitt and Minn could hardly contain their excitement when the back gate of the truck was lifted and the cows began to step out. Both mice chattered to Lilka, in the way that very happy mice will do, that they wanted to find Viktor right away and ask him where their parents were living. Minn imagined her parents living on a farm as pretty as the Nelson Farm. She began to think how nice it would be that, once they found them there, they could all live happily ever after in a setting as lovely as this one.

The cows walked single file into the longest of the white barns, each stepping into a neat stall. The floors were painted a soft gray color and the stall doors were painted white with red trim. There were silver buckets of all sizes sitting on a long shelf that ran along the far wall, and each one was shinier than a new silver coin. Farmer Nelson made sure each Jersey cow had a good breakfast of summer grass, and then he left in the quiet way that he had arrived, closing the barn door behind him.

The moment he did, Mitt and Minn sprang from hiding and rushed to Lilka. "Where is Viktor? We must talk to him right away!"

Lilka called for Viktor in the way an old cow will call for a mouse. Viktor was an Eastern wood rat and an uncommon type of mouse for the area. He had settled at the Nelson Farm years before, and he found it a good place to stay. There were always tiny things for him to collect and put in his nest. He found coins and marbles, hairpins and gumballs. One time he even found a small magnifying glass and put it near his bed. He pushed it upright against a nearby wall, and the next morning when he woke up he looked straight through it and saw very large cows. He scared himself so much that he hid the glass and never took anything like that again. When the cows asked him what happened to the spyglass, Viktor, not known for telling the truth at all times, told them another wood rat must have taken it and carried it far away.

As Lilka kept calling for Viktor, Minn decided to tour the barn. She walked the edge of the shelf with the silver buckets, going behind them to search for crumbs. She was very careful, paying attention not to get too near to them. Mitt stayed near Lilka, turning his face from side to side to see if Viktor was coming.

Minn was behind one bucket when all of a sudden—CRASH! The buckets started falling off the shelf one-by-one, beginning at the farthest end. Minn had no idea why this was happening, and so she jumped

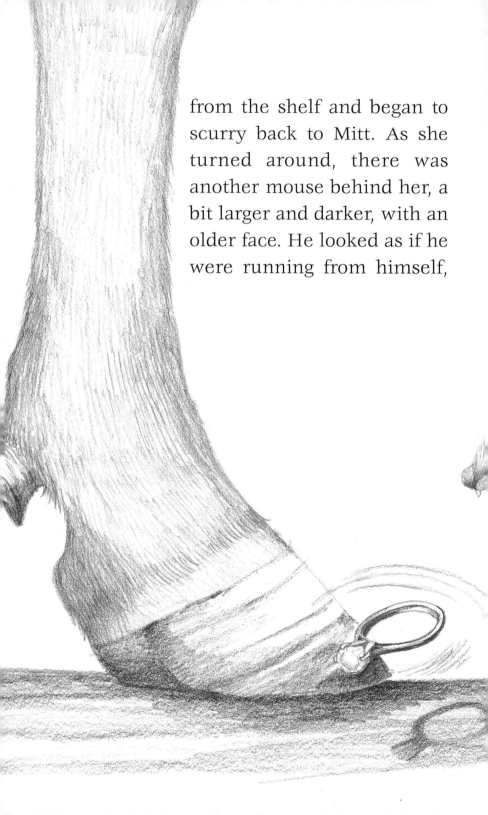

from the shelf and began to scurry back to Mitt. As she turned around, there was another mouse behind her, a bit larger and darker, with an older face. He looked as if he were running from himself, carrying a diamond ring in his mouth. He ran straight to Lilka, unaware of Minn's presence. When he reached the Jersey cow, he came to a sudden halt, dropping the ring at her feet.

CHAPTER THREE

Viktor

"Viktor!" Lilka cried out, in the way a surprised cow will do. "Where have you been and what have you taken now?"

Viktor began to explain that he had been in Farmer Nelson's home and in his pantry. He said he spotted the shiny object in a little dish on top of the sugar canister, and he couldn't help but take it with him. His whiskers twitched as he spoke, for his heart was still rushing with fright. He continued to explain to Lilka that Farmer Nelson had opened the pantry door and spotted him. He had to run as fast as he could out the knothole in the front door and into the barnyard, past the chickens, and into the barn.

"Why, Viktor," said Lilka, "that must be Mrs. Nelson's wedding ring from long ago. He misses her very much. You must return that at once."

Lilka was so busy scolding Viktor that she forgot all about Mitt and Minn and their quest for their parents. Viktor was unaware of the guests, too, until he took notice of something behind Lilka. As he did, Lilka remembered the mice and changed the subject. "Viktor, these are Mitt and Minn. I met them at the Cheese

Jamboree. They are looking for their parents, and I think you may know where their parents are living."

Viktor crept closer, nosing in on Minn. He put his face to hers, and then he turned to look at Mitt.

"They look just like them!" laughed Viktor. "Spitting images, both of them."

Mitt and Minn wanted to believe him. But after all they had seen and heard so far, they didn't know if he was telling the truth. A dark feeling came over Mitt that maybe Viktor was fibbing and knew nothing about their parents.

As the four of them stood quietly in the barn, Minn stepped away from Mitt and went front and center to Viktor. She drew a deep breath and spoke, "Do you really know our parents?"

"Why, yes," he snorted. "I said so, didn't I?"

"Then, where are they?" responded Minn. Viktor settled himself into a tuft of hay beside Lilka's foot, the stolen ring still nearby.

"Your parents came here by mistake. Your mother told how long ago you all were living in a nest tucked into discarded barn boards out in the middle of the forest. One evening, a bobcat had discovered the nest and was making his hungry intentions known, and so she had to take you children from the nest and place you in safe spots away from any danger, because that is what white-footed mice will do in times of trouble. Your father stayed at the nest while your mother moved you one by one, and after she was sure that each of you was safe and sound, she and your father were squeezing their way out of the barn boards. In an instant, the two of them were scooped into a pile of debris and dropped into an old truck. Your mother said that, at that moment, the truck drove away, taking them and the barn boards with it. Three days later they showed up here, drenched

from rain and frightened by thunder and lightning. The truck had come here to deliver old boards to Mr. Nelson, so he could use them for making old-fashioned picture frames."

Mitt and Minn were interested in the story, but yet did not totally believe Viktor. "So, how do you know it was them?" huffed Mitt.

"Well, I can tell by just looking at you," replied Viktor.

"Oh, you can, can you?" snarled Mitt, now impatient and tired and swelling with disbelief. "I don't believe a word that you are saying."

Viktor turned away and scrambled into his nest, which was tucked into the far corner of Lilka's stall. Moments later he was back with a long piece of red wool yarn in his mouth.

"Your mother gave me this. She said she grabbed it before she was dropped out of the truck. It's from your nest."

Mitt and Minn nosed in on the yarn, sniffing it, mouthing it, and exploring it in all the ways that mice will explore. As Mitt did, he could smell the sweet scent of his mother. He could almost hear her voice singing to him in the warm snug nest they had shared long ago. Minn also could tell it belonged to their mother, as the yarn was the exact shade of red as the mitten that Gerdie had saved from the basket of cherries.

Mitt and Minn felt badly that they had doubted Viktor. Mitt spoke first, "Can you tell us where they are? Can you help us get there?"

Viktor replied in a halfhearted manner, insulted by their initial lack of trust. "I can tell you where they are. They are living on a farm not far from here. I could take you there if you want me to."

Mitt and Minn wanted Viktor to lead them to the farm right away. Mitt's heart was bursting with longing for his parents, and Minn felt a gentle warmth sweeping over her that reminded her of quiet nights in Gerdie's cabin, tucked in a teacup and nibbling on oatmeal cookie crumbs.

"So let's go," urged Mitt, thanking Lilka for her help as he nudged Viktor toward the barn door.

Just then, the barn door opened. As it swung wide, Mitt, Minn, Viktor, and Lilka watched as Farmer Nelson walked inside, a handkerchief in his hands. The corners of his eyes were glistening not from joy or laughter, but from the wetness of tears. He nosed around the barn a bit as if looking for something, and then sadly wiped his face with the handkerchief and slowly walked out.

Lilka spoke first and directly to the wood rat. "You must return the diamond ring to the house before you go, Viktor. You must do that or I will not let you return to your nest. Ever."

With that, Lilka stomped her foot and Viktor tried to peek around it, looking at his home where all his special treasures were stored. Viktor spoke to Mitt and Minn. "If you help me return the ring safely, then I will take you to your parents."

Minn looked at Mitt. She tried to read the soft look on his face and, from it, she knew that Mitt was afraid and disappointed at the same time. Even so, Mitt said nothing of his feelings to Minn. Instead, he told Minn that they must help Viktor. Not only because they had insulted Viktor when he was telling the truth, but because if the wood rat did not return from the farmer's house safely, they would never find their parents.

There was no other choice in the matter.

CHAPTER FOUR
Henka

Night fell upon the farm in the long and lazy way a late summer night will fall. The faraway chorus frogs began to sing, while the night air gently teased the tall field grasses into a dance. The air was heavy with the scent of water and still hot from the day so the mice were moving slowly.

"We must first go quietly up to the house and in through the knothole at the back screen door," whispered Viktor. Mitt and Minn followed him across the barnyard and up to the entrance. They slipped in quietly and huddled together on the inside so that Viktor could tell them the rest of the plan. But first, he had to warn them about Henka.

Henka was the farmer's house cat, and she didn't like mice. Nervously, Mitt and Minn followed Viktor through the kitchen and toward the pantry door. It was slightly

open and, as Viktor nosed it more open, the door squeaked. It squeaked only a little, and it did not wake the farmer who was sleeping in a bedroom nearby.

Instead, it woke Henka. All at once, the kitchen was a flurry of three mice trying to outrun the well-fed black-and-white tabby cat. Her stubby paws were swiping the air as she pounced for the mice. The three split in different directions to confuse the cat. Viktor was on the sugar canister near the dish with the wedding ring in his mouth when, all of a sudden, MEOW! Henka cornered Viktor in the pantry.

Viktor dropped the ring in the dish as he had planned. He looked straight at Henka, who muttered to him in a low cat tone, "Why, Viktor, I never knew that fear had such big eyes. Watch closely now, because I'm going to eat you!"

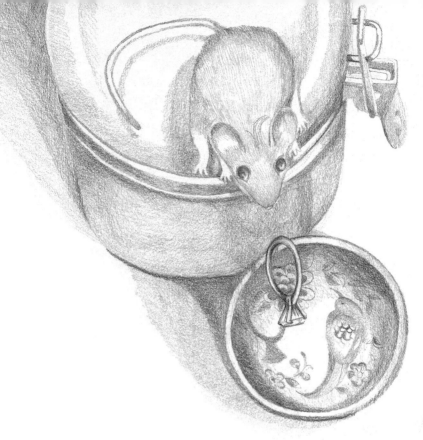

Henka pounced upon Viktor. Mitt wanted to run away and stay safe, and yet he wanted to help Viktor at the same time. Minn could not tell if she wanted Viktor to live because he was a good mouse, or if she wanted him to live because he was their only hope of finding their parents. Being kind of heart, no matter how it may hurt them, Mitt and Minn decided they should both help save Viktor.

Mitt spotted a shelf over the window with the same type of shiny silver pails that were in the barn. Remembering how much noise they made when they fell, he jumped up on the shelf and looked at Minn.

Minn knew just what to do. She ran to Henka's backside and pulled the cat's tail. When the cat turned around to yowl at the disturbance, Mitt knocked a pail off the shelf and it fell right over Henka's head.

The cat was angry now that her head was in a pail, and she began to spin around in circles. As she did, the three ran out of the house and into the yard. They hid in the rose garden, where it was dark enough to remain unseen. As they waited to catch their breaths, in the slight glow from the moonlight, they saw a figure lurking in front of the barn door. It was Henka. And she looked mad. Really mad.

CHAPTER FIVE

Lunt

The three knew they could not return to
the barn because Henka was waiting for
them. They must start out for the farm two
roads away where Mitt and Minn's parents

were living. It was night and there was danger. But what choice did they have?

Viktor urged Mitt and Minn to follow him quickly from the rose garden to the water pump at the edge of the farm. When they reached the pump, Viktor told them they must run quickly through the meadow and to the edge of the first road.

Mitt and Minn followed Viktor through a series of paths that traced through the meadow. Just as they reached the edge of the first road, a large silent shadow cast a blanket of total darkness in the night sky above them. It was Lunt, and she was on the move.

Lunt was a great horned owl and she lived in an abandoned red-tailed hawk's nest at the edge of the meadow. She saw the three mice racing across the field and flew in to snatch them just as they reached the road.

She was circling now. Once. Twice.

Minn tried to hide in the tall meadow grasses, burrowing herself deep in their blades, while Mitt and Viktor hid behind a nearby field stone.

Lunt landed on the ground between them and looked from left to right. The moonlight washed the summer meadow in shades of gold, and Lunt's eyes reflected the blaze of her hunger. Which one to eat first?

As Lunt began to reach for Minn, something parted the grasses. It was coming their way and it was very large. It was Henka.

CHAPTER SIX

Schwindler Brothers Farm

Lunt spotted the cat as quickly as the cat spotted Lunt. Their eyes locked and Lunt decided that perhaps the cat would be a better dinner. In a flash of wings and fur, Lunt was chasing Henka through the meadow.

As the three mice watched them disappear, Minn spoke first. "So much for the owl and the pussycat, wouldn't you say?"

The three laughed as they made their way across the road and into the forest. When they reached the second road, not far from the farm, they stopped to wait for an old work truck that was sputtering down the dirt road. It had one headlight missing and the tailgate was rattling. As the three made their way closer to the farm, the sky moved from deep of night to early morning, the time when darkness was fading yet morning light was not yet rising. The sky was a smoky haze of dark blue and gray as they reached their destination.

"Well, this is it," exclaimed Viktor. "This is where your parents are living."

The farm did not look anything like the Nelson farm. It was a simple farm with one barn that was leaning badly to the right side, the boards in need of new paint and nails. The fence around the pen beside the barn was rusty and broken in many places. Although they had yet to see any hogs, the scent told them it was a hog farm. Mitt noticed the barn must have been in better shape a long time ago. There was a plaque on the side of the barn that read "Schwindler Brothers Farm—Happy Healthy Hogs." But those letters were crossed out with paint, and beneath them new words spelled out something else: Schwindler Brothers Farm—Fat Lazy Pigs.

Mitt began to weep. His heart felt heavy for his parents, as he couldn't bear to think about how terrible it must be for them to live here.

Mitt jumped at Viktor. He couldn't wait any longer to see his mother and father, and Minn was just as desperate. "Where are they, Viktor? Can you bring us to them now?"

The sun was getting a bit higher in the morning sky now, and the Duroc hogs were starting to stir about the barnyard. They were, indeed, fat, lazy pigs, thought Mitt. Their ears were hanging low upon their faces, and their bellies were soft and caked with old dry mud. They walked slowly to the discarded bathtub that was their food trough, filled and ready for them, and began to snort and forage and fill their faces with a morning meal.

Viktor looked at the barnyard. It seemed as if there were twice as many hogs as last time he was here. Viktor counted as they filled the pen—thirty, forty, fifty—then came medium-sized pigs, and among the sows and boars were piglets running here and there. Viktor stopped counting at one hundred and twelve. Minn tightened her ears to her head to muffle the noise of their snorting and sniffing, and Mitt was growing impatient with Viktor.

But just then, the sea of hogs parted to the far sides of the pen as a large grayish-black goose waded through them. The goose walked slowly, its body nearly skimming the ground and its wings darting out here and there to help it stay balanced. The goose was Quinby, a Toulouse goose, gentle in nature. Quinby spotted Viktor and his companions right away and nosed in on Minn, sensing she needed some ribbing.

"Do you know how to get down from a horse?" asked Quinby.

Minn stammered a bit, not knowing what to say, but then she quietly said, "No, I'm sorry. I don't."

Quinby laughed. "That's right, old friend, because you don't get down from a horse, you get down from a goose!" And with that Quinby turned in a complete circle and plopped herself down amidst the three of them.

Mitt could not wait any longer. "Where are our parents?"

"Your parents?" asked the goose.

"Yes, our parents," said Mitt, in a straight and serious tone.

Quinby looked confused and Viktor stepped in to explain. Viktor told Quinby the story of Mitt, how he lost his mitten, and how he had traveled everywhere to find it. He told how Minn had traveled as well and, when the pair met at the Cheese Jamboree in Wisconsin, they had discovered they were sister and brother. Viktor told about Lilka and how she met them at the Jamboree and told them she knew where their parents were. He finished by telling Quinby that he had brought them here so they could be together with their parents at last.

Quinby straightened her neck and pulled her goose face downward in a serious manner. Then she stretched her neck out to Mitt and Minn and said the saddest words the pair ever thought they could hear.

"Your parents are gone."

CHAPTER SEVEN

Fat, Lazy Pigs

Mitt and Minn began to sob, thinking the worst. Perhaps the barn was too messy and there wasn't enough food for them to survive? Perhaps there were too many sows and boars and they were stepped on? Perhaps …

"You just missed them. They left this morning," continued Quinby.

Quinby invited the mice into the barn to explain how their parents had left because the barn repairman was here last night and said the barn could not be saved and would have to be torn down. She told Mitt and Minn that a truck left early that morning for Chicago, and their parents thought perhaps they could make a new start in the big city.

Mitt and Minn looked around the barn, which was the filthiest barn they had ever seen. In the midst of it, they noticed one old photograph hanging on the wall. It was a beautiful healthy boar and beneath the picture it said "Schwindler's Sweet Delight. Grand Champion 1905."

Quinby explained. "Long ago this farm belonged to the Schwindler family. It was a tidy farm with red hogs, white hogs, and spotted hogs. A cleaner farm there never was. Sweet Delight was the grandest champion that ever lived. He won every blue ribbon at the state fair, and every gold championship cup. He was strong and meaty, but kind in nature and never boastful about his good fortune. Then came the piglets of Sweet Delight. They were not so bad, but then came his children's children. With every generation, each litter thought they were more entitled to grand rewards than ever before. These young pigs ate much. They slept much. They grew soft and muddy and greedy. And so did the children of the Schwindler family. Now all that are left are two Schwindler brothers, and they can barely afford to keep the farm running. Soon it will be over, as the barn must be torn down and the pigs sent away. That's why your parents had to leave."

Mitt and Minn looked out over the barnyard. A lazier group of pigs they had never seen. Although Mitt and Minn were sad

their parents were not here at the Schwindler Farm, they were relieved they were not living in such a horrible place. But now as the daylight was burning, Mitt and Minn had to figure out how to get to Chicago.

Viktor, who had grown to like Mitt and Minn very much, told them that tomorrow there would be two trucks arriving in the early morning. He told the mice that one delivers feed, the other delivers seed. Both trucks are marked. One says: FEED. The other says: SEED. The feed truck is from Chicago, which is directly east. The seed truck is from the south.

All Mitt and Minn had to do now was hide in the feed truck when it arrived and take it to Chicago tomorrow morning. It would not be hard to do.

At least that's what they thought.

GRAND CHAMPION

1905

Schwindler's
Sweet Delight
Grand Champion 1905

CHAPTER EIGHT

Feed and Seed

Mitt and Minn woke when they heard the trucks arrive. They came earlier than Viktor thought. It was so early in the morning that it seemed to be more like the middle of the night. The moon was covered by the clouds, making it very dark outside. The trucks were similar, so Mitt and Minn paid close attention to the letters on the sides of each.

This was going to be easy. The drivers were in the house settling up with the Schwindler brothers and the back door to the feed truck was wide open. Viktor and Quinby stood nearby as Mitt and Minn climbed into the back of the feed truck and settled in unnoticed. Moments later, the driver closed the tailgate and drove away.

Still half asleep and weary, Viktor asked with a start, "Quinby, did I tell them feed or seed?"

Quinby poked at Viktor, knowing that this question meant that Viktor had sent them away on the wrong truck.

Hours later, the feed truck pulled to a stop. It was late morning and so Mitt and Minn thought they must be close to Chicago. The pair hopped out and raced down the street, their paws moving as fast as their hearts were wishing them to run. But, as the pair turned the first corner and raced headlong into a park, it was clear. This was not Chicago.

"Mitt," cried Minn, "where are we? This is not a city of skyscrapers and towers and cars and people. Where could we be?" Mitt did not want Minn to know that he was afraid they were lost, but his lowered ears must have told her so.

Before they had a chance to say more, a crush of people flooded into the park where Mitt and Minn were standing. The people quickly began to sit at the picnic tables, each person opening brown paper sacks or white canvas bags. They were laughing and smiling, pulling out wedges of cheddar cheese and thick seeded crackers. They had all sorts of treats, such as laces of red licorice and bags of potato chips.

All at once Mitt and Minn realized how hungry they were and waited under one of the tables for crumbs to drop. One of the tourists had set her canvas bag on the lawn beneath the table and both mice crawled into it, enticed by the smell of the grapes and chocolate cookies packed inside. The pair forgot all about their troubles as they moved about the bag, eating and resting, nibbling and dozing.

With so much comfort and food, the pair quickly fell asleep. When it was time for

the tourists to leave, the woman picked up
her bag and slung it around her arm. Now
Mitt and Minn were trapped inside, with
no way out.

CHAPTER NINE

The Land of Lincoln

Lincolns Home in Springfield Illinois

The woman joined a line of visitors and walked into a building. They were chatting with each other about Old Abe and how lovely it was to visit Springfield, Illinois, this time of year.

Mitt tried to listen and, in the simple way that a white-footed mouse can understand things, tried to figure out what they were

saying. Before Mitt and Minn could learn any more about where they were, the woman dropped her bag, spilling the contents everywhere. She reached to grab the rolling grapes and chocolate cookies before they made a mess in the home of Abraham Lincoln, and the distraction allowed Mitt and Minn a chance to escape. The pair scurried up a wall of bookshelves to rest at the very top, out of sight from the visitors.

The sound of footsteps coming in and out of the room all day provided a low, steady rhythm that lulled Mitt and Minn into a long sleep. Long after the last visitor left the Lincoln home, Mitt and Minn were still sleeping on the shelf, unaware of how much time had passed.

The clock chimed twelve times and midnight arrived. Minn woke first, feeling as if someone was staring at her in her sleep.

And someone was.

"Hello, there." The tall thin gentleman greeted Minn in a formal way, nodding his head slightly and keeping one hand in his vest pocket. "I hope you have found my home warm and suitable for your resting pleasure," he added.

With that, he held both mice in his hands and walked to the kitchen table where he lit the lamp and poured himself a cup of tea. He placed the pair in the center of the table and let them talk to him, much in the way a pair of mice waking in the middle of the night can talk to a stranger.

The conversation warmed Minn, as it reminded her of her life with Gerdie in Minnesota. Mitt was awake, too, now that the aroma of the tea roused him. Before long, the pair was telling their story to the kind gentleman. Mitt went first, explaining how he had been searching for his home for a very long time and that he and his sister were trying very hard to find their parents. Minn told all about her journey, too, and how she ached to see her mother again, not just her mouse mother but Gerdie, the woman from Ely who had been her mother, too.

The man smiled and, in a smooth tone of voice, told them that he understood about how love for a mother can be. "All that I am," he said, "or hope to be, I owe to my angel mother."

Right then Mitt and Minn knew that he understood their tale, and they thought perhaps he could help them find their way to Chicago. So they asked him for help.

The gentleman looked out the window before responding to their request. He said, "That is my horse, Old Bob. He is a good horse. He will take you to Chicago."

Mitt and Minn joined him looking out the window. It seemed like a fine idea, but Mitt worried that they would not get there soon enough to find their parents before winter set in.

Minn disagreed. "The horse will be plenty fast, and what other choice do we have, Mitt?" Minn was upset with Mitt right now, and she let her feelings show.

Mitt had little patience for his sister at the moment, so he came at her full charge.

"What do you know? All you do is tag along and follow anyway. I'm the one in the front trying to find the way."

Minn huffed and turned her back toward Mitt.

But then the nice man spoke. "Ah, now, you may take my horse, but you must remember this—a mouse divided against itself will not stand."

Nobody had ever spoken to them in such a firm way or offered them such a fine piece of advice. Mitt and Minn knew that he was right. They quickly made amends and spent the rest of the night talking with the man at the kitchen table. The moment the sun rose, he told them Old Bob was ready and waiting for them. As they scrambled out the door, he said, "You can call me Abe."

With that, Mitt said good-bye and Minn spoke back to the man, "What a pleasant home you have, Abe. Thank you!"

The pair ran out of the house and across the front lawn toward the horse. As they did, Mitt stopped to read a sign, slowly and letter-by-letter in the way a small mouse will read. It said "Home of Abraham Lincoln. Born 1809, Died 1865. 16th President of the United States."

The pair stood still. How could that be? Was he real? They stood there in disbelief and then they remembered Old Bob. It seemed that now, after all they had been through, they had a good way to reach Chicago.

That is, if Old Bob was real.

CHAPTER TEN
Mikko and Okko

Mitt and Minn ran to the front of the gate where Old Bob was said to be standing. Even though they were now unsure whether Old Bob existed, they had to try to find him because he would be their only way to Chicago. They did not see Gamel standing there. Gamel was a very old common raccoon and he was hungry. He was used to nourishing himself with tidbits that tourists left behind, but today, he was hungry for a mouse.

As Mitt and Minn ran by, Gamel reached out and grabbed Minn with his mouth. He held her there gently, wondering if he should try to take the other mouse, too. But instead, he simply turned around and began to run back to his home in a nearby woodshed.

Mitt began to call nervously for Minn. He followed Gamel, hoping to reach him before Minn was gone for good. But then, Mitt heard a loud laughing call from above—Ka-lah-lak! Ka-lah-lak! Gamel heard it, too, and stopped to listen. Ka-lah-lak! Ka-lah-lak!

Just then two greater white-fronted geese descended upon Gamel, using their bright orange legs to bump him around a bit, just enough to make him drop the mouse. This was an unusual thing for such small geese to do, but after chasing Gamel away they introduced themselves to Mitt and Minn.

"We are Mikko and Okko, friends of Quinby's. We often stop to feed on corn where Quinby lives. We are on our way south, and Quinby told us that Viktor placed you on the wrong truck. We are glad that we found you."

"Are you here to take us to Chicago?" asked Minn.

"Yes," said Okko. She was a very ladylike goose. She had been Mikko's mate for several years. The pair never traveled anywhere without the other. They were grayish in color, with spotted chests and pink bills. Minn thought Okko was lovely and kind.

"We will take you to Chicago, but first we must follow the river southward a bit to meet up with the rest of our formation. When we find them, we will all escort you to Chicago before returning to our southward path."

65

Mitt and Minn began to cheer. They would finally reach Chicago and find their parents.

"Climb up," said Mikko to Mitt. Minn climbed up onto Okko as well. Each mouse held on tight to the dense under feathers of each bird and the pair of geese lofted up and high into the late summer sky.

Mikko and Okko flew southwestward, catching air currents when possible, gently gliding not too far from the ground. Mitt and Minn both enjoyed the scenery very much, the gently rolling fields of green and brown giving way to prairies and, later, shallow marshes and bays along the river. Mikko and Okko would stop often, searching for grains to eat in marshy areas. Mitt and Minn enjoyed this part, too, for they were able to forage for nuts and berries alongside the wetlands.

When the geese reached the Mississippi River, they began to follow it southward to the Mark Twain National Wildlife Refuge. This was where they would meet the others, Okko said. But when they landed, the others were not there.

Mitt and Minn quickly scrambled into the dense weeds and rushes, searching for good things to eat while Mikko and Okko called for the others. Wa-wa-wa! Wa-wa-wa! This was a different sound than Mitt had heard before and, in it, he could tell Mikko and Okko were worried about the others. Mitt and Minn wanted to get to Chicago more than anything, but now they had to wait.

"Can't we just leave without them?" begged Minn.

"No," said Okko, in a calm, motherly tone. "We must all fly together. We will be going off course, and the only way to survive is to depend upon one another."

Mitt was listening. He understood. He hoped that Minn did, too. In the middle of the refuge, while great blue herons waded in the shallows and solitary sandpipers went fleeting around the water's edge, Mitt and Minn had no choice but to settle into a nest with Mikko and Okko and wait. The four watched and waited for days, but the others did not arrive. Mikko tried to hide his fear from Okko, hoping not to cause her worry.

But Mitt and Minn knew something had happened. Something terrible. And Mitt was angry, both that something terrible had happened and that it was ruining his plans. Then he felt bad for feeling so selfish.

One morning, Mitt woke Minn and nudged her out of the nest while the geese were still sleeping. He could sense the weather changing and the air growing colder. He knew they could not wait any longer. "We will have to go on our own," Mitt told Minn.

Minn agreed and, as the sun was starting to edge its way above the horizon, coaxing white-throated sparrows and dark-eyed juncos out of their dreams, the pair set off to make a new plan.

But in an instant—WHOOSH! In came a golden eagle, grabbing both mice, one in each talon. The eagle was Ragnar and he was hungry.

CHAPTER ELEVEN
Ragnar

Ragnar held each mouse so firmly in his grasp that neither could move. Mitt didn't like seeing the scared look on Minn's face, and Minn didn't like knowing that Mitt was noticing her fear. Ragnar was not a gentle flyer, either, as he flew to the Illinois River and began to follow it southward. The two mice, wanting nothing more than to find their parents, began to believe they never would.

Ragnar followed the great river south, the craggy bluffs below looking large and steep as he lofted downward toward them, roosting in a clutch of pignut hickory trees on a cliff just north of Alton. Mitt could tell the air was a bit cooler than it had been when their journey began. Sitting in the tops of the trees, he noticed that the leaves were just starting to turn from bright green to soft yellow.

Ragnar settled in and squeezed the mice just to make sure he had their attention as he was preparing to eat them.

Just as Ragnar's beak was about to open, a bald eagle came lashing in at Ragnar, pushing his talons into Ragnar's wings. The bald eagle had claimed the area for the coming winter. It upset him to see Ragnar there, and so he decided to defend his claim. Ragnar was caught off guard by the surprise attack and let go of Mitt and Minn, who tumbled downward through the branches of the old hickory, each limb slowing their fall as they fell down.

When they reached the forest floor, both Mitt and Minn were stunned. The pair was in desperate need of a few moments to catch their breaths when, all of a sudden, they were grabbed by the tails and scooped up into the air.

It was a big brown bat and he wasn't letting go.

CHAPTER TWELVE

Taavi

The big brown bat was Taavi. He had been sleeping in a bark crevice in the hickory tree when Mitt and Minn's noisy tumble woke him.

Taavi had their tails in his small mouth and he was winging toward a small funnel-like opening in the side of a cliff. It seemed to

be a small cave of sorts, and Mitt and Minn thought it was the end. Once the bat brought them into the cave, thought Mitt, they would never see daylight again.

Taavi flitted awkwardly into the opening. The cave was much darker inside than it was outside at dusk. Mitt and Minn recognized the chirping sounds of phoebe birds nesting in the walls of the cave and heard a deafening chorus of crickets coming from further inside the cave. Taavi landed on a rocky ledge within the cave, gently putting Mitt and Minn down upon it.

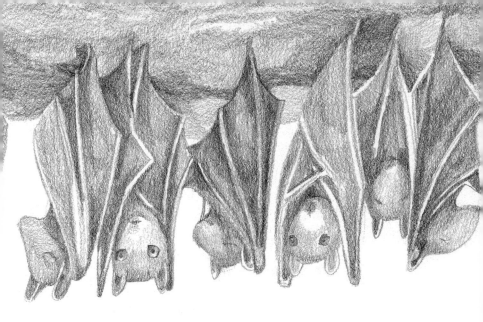

"You don't know how close you were to being dinner, my friends."

Mitt and Minn didn't know what to say. Did it mean the bat was going to eat them for dinner but had changed his mind to save them for breakfast instead? Mitt and Minn stood silent.

"You didn't see him?" quizzed Taavi. "I saved you! Two steps away from where you landed sat a striped skunk. It almost ate you!"

Mitt and Minn had no idea about the skunk, but were now more interested in why the bat had taken them into the cave.

"Are you going to eat us?" asked Minn, in a very soft, sad sort of way.

Taavi began to laugh. "Are you kidding? Big brown bats don't eat mice, we eat moths. I'm not going to eat you—not now, not ever."

Mitt and Minn relaxed a bit, although they were not too thrilled at being in such a dark cave. "Then what are you going to do with us?" asked Mitt.

"Nothing," replied Taavi. "I saved you and now I'm done with you."

Mitt was confused. "You see," said Taavi, "bats are gentle creatures. We aren't bad, we're just misunderstood."

Mitt and Minn's eyes were adjusting to the dark cave now, and they were able to see around them. The ceiling of the cave was covered with bats just like Taavi, each of them hanging quietly, sometimes stretching their wings and nodding their heads, a few beginning to wake and move around, ready to leave for the evening.

Mitt began to worry. How would they get out of the cave? No matter where he looked, he saw bats and rocks and birds and salamanders. He didn't see an opening. He didn't see any light. No matter how hard he looked, he saw no way out of the cave.

CHAPTER THIRTEEN
The Piasa

Before Mitt could say anything, Taavi asked them if they knew of the Piasa.

Mitt answered no. Minn shook her head. Neither Mitt nor Minn was in the mood for a tale. But neither wanted to be rude to Taavi after he had saved them from a hungry skunk.

"You see, long ago there was a horrible creature that lived in Illinois. It was larger than a bear, and part bird and part dragon. It had long wings covered in scales and a tail that whipped back and forth with a sharp end to it. It had eyes full of flames, sharp teeth, and two horns. It was called the Piasa."

Mitt and Minn leaned in. Minn looked over her shoulder to make sure nothing was lurking there.

Taavi continued. "The Piasa was horrible and mean, and liked to frighten every creature in its path—even humans. One day, a great chief had enough of the Piasa, so he set a trap for it. He called for twenty braves with arrows to come along with him and wait in hiding in the bluffs above the river." Mitt thought about that. He had seen the bluffs and the river, so he knew the story must be true.

"The chief was very brave. He stepped out into the open and called for the Piasa to come and get him. When the Piasa came flying his way, the braves jumped out from the bluffs and shot arrows up at his wings. The Piasa screamed loudly and flew away. Most think the Piasa did not live."

Then Taavi leaned in and whispered, "I think it's still out there. I've seen it."

"Oh, Taavi," a scolding voice echoed from behind. "What in the world are you doing?" It was Taavi's mother. She looked just like Taavi but was much bigger and heavier. She looked at Mitt and Minn with kindness. Then, she gave Taavi a stern face. "Taavi, you can't keep telling mice that you are rescuing them from a skunk, just so you can bring them back here to tell them stories all night." She looked at the mice and said, "Don't believe a word he says," and flew away.

Mitt and Minn were a little cross with Taavi for making them believe they were almost eaten by a skunk, but now they didn't know whether or not there really was a Piasa.

Taavi was on the ledge folded up as small as he could make himself. He was ashamed he had tricked them into thinking they were almost eaten by a skunk just so he could impress them. He hoped his new friends wouldn't think less of him.

Minn understood how Taavi was feeling. Mitt noticed, too, and spoke up. "Taavi, will you let us tell you a story?" Taavi was happy that the mice were not angry with him.

So there in the darkness, upon a cool flat ledge in a cave, Mitt told Taavi the whole story of their journey from start to end. Minn tried hard not to cry, but hearing the story all over again made her feel even more eager to get to Chicago.

Taavi wanted to make up for tricking them. He wanted to show that he truly was a helpful creature. Quickly, he grabbed Mitt and Minn by their tails and carried them out of the cave and into the night sky, winging his way southward along the river. It was not easy. Taavi worked hard to fly and keep hold of their tails at the same time. As they flew through the night sky, they passed a cliff.

And there it was. On the side of the cliff was a creature—half bird, half dragon. It was an image of the Piasa and it looked just like Taavi had described. Minn closed her eyes and Mitt began to gasp. Taavi flew as fast as he could. Perhaps, thought Mitt, the legend was true.

CHAPTER FOURTEEN
Chicago

Taavi worked hard to bring the pair into the Shawnee National Wilderness. It was almost morning by the time he got there. Because it was nearly light, he dropped them upon a forest road, knowing there would be bikers from Chicago riding along the dirt road, and that with them Mitt and Minn would find their way to the city.

The bat left quickly and, before Mitt and Minn knew what was happening, a large group of bikers came whirring toward them, dust spitting out from behind their tires.

Mitt and Minn would never have time to scramble out of the way. The tires were narrowly missing Mitt and Minn, who were separated in the crush of bikes. One bike went over Mitt's tail, injuring him and pinning him to the ground for a moment. Minn tried to rush to his side, but too many bicycles were still rushing by.

"Mitt," cried Minn. "Mitt, where are you?"

Mitt did not answer.

Minn hollered again. "Mitt, where are you?"

There was still no answer. It was quiet now and the riders had passed. All that remained was a cloud of dust, which was slowly starting to settle toward the ground.

Minn kept calling, but even so, there was no answer from Mitt. Minn began to weep. As she sat in the middle of the trail, she didn't notice the riders who had come up from behind her. They were two children— a boy and a girl.

"Oh, look!" said the girl. "A mouse. It's hurt. It's not moving."

With that, the little girl picked up Minn and put her in her bike basket. Minn was so stunned she could barely move. She had to find Mitt. She couldn't leave without him. But the girl rode away, taking Minn with her.

Just then, Mitt began to call, "Minn, Minn!" It was a quiet call from Mitt, who was stunned and resting in the ditch not far from where Minn had been. He had been tossed into the ditch by the wheel of a bike, and it took him several minutes to regain his breath.

"Minn!" he called again, in the sharp way that a hurt, frightened mouse will call. "Minn, where are you?"

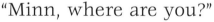

But there was no answer.

Mitt called for his sister again. But no matter how many times he cried out to her, there was still no answer. Mitt crawled out to the roadside, nursing his injured tail. He looked from left to right. There were no bikes. There was no more dust. There was no more Minn.

Mitt had not heard the young girl and boy who came behind the other riders. He did not know that Minn had been picked up and carried away. He thought Minn had been crushed in the pack of bicycles, so he went back into the ditch and began to cry.

What would he tell Gerdie, he thought? And then Mitt's thoughts went a bit deeper. What would he tell his parents?

Meanwhile, the young girl and boy caught up with their parents and packed their bikes to start for home. The girl had already made a bed for Minn in an old cooler they had brought along with them. She put holes in the cover and grasses in the bottom. Although it was a comfortable place to be, Minn did not like being caged in such a manner.

The sunlight was fading as the family traveled north in their car. At the same time, the sun was beginning to set in the forest. Mitt found refuge in a rotted stump, not far from the edge of the road. The sounds of white-tailed deer starting to browse in the forest shrubs and the footsteps of wild turkey foraging in the understory soothed Mitt into a very deep and dreamless sleep. The family kept driving through the night until they reached their home.

That's when Minn heard one word she had been waiting to hear for a very long time. "Okay, kids, we're back home in Chicago!"

Chicago, thought Minn. I'm in Chicago! Minn could not believe her ears. Chicago, she thought. I'm here. But her happiness quickly turned to tears when she thought about being in Chicago without Mitt. This is not the way it was supposed to be. This is not the way the story should end, thought Minn. I will find our parents. I know I will.

CHAPTER FIFTEEN
Trula

When Mitt awoke the next morning, a rush of sadness overcame him. Minn is gone. I am alone. I must make it to Chicago no matter what, he thought. I will find our parents and tell them all about her. Mitt remembered how Gerdie was so selfless in letting Minn go along with him. He remembered how Gerdie wanted Minn to go back home with her and live happily in Ely. He remembered how Gerdie pointed to the words on the poster at the Cheese Jamboree. All Heart. Do Try.

And that's when Mitt found his courage. All Heart. Do Try.

I have to try, thought Mitt. I can't give up now. Minn is gone for good, but I will make her proud.

Mitt raced out of the stump and began to make his way through the forest. He knew of the dangers overhead, as turkey vultures and kestral hawks were eyeing him. He was paying close attention to the dangers in the sky when—WHAM! A paw came down on top of him. Everything was dark.

It was Soren. The coyote was waiting for a snack like Mitt to come along. He held Mitt to the ground but, this time, Mitt fought back. He squirmed and he wriggled and he nipped at Soren's paw, causing the coyote to yelp and lift his paw just enough for Mitt to escape.

But this did only one thing; it made Soren very, very angry.

Soren began to chase Mitt as Mitt tried very hard to lose the lean coyote. The mouse dashed forward, while Soren was only steps behind. With every step he seemed to be getting closer. Mitt thought it was the end.

◆

Meanwhile, Minn was trying very hard to find a way out of the cage that had been made for her. She was so sad about losing Mitt that she didn't eat, and she didn't move around very much. The next morning she heard the father say, "I think this mouse is sick and I should take it to see Dr. Johnston."

Minn didn't move.

The father went on, "The mouse isn't eating or drinking and it barely moves. We better find out what is wrong and help her."

Within moments, the father was lifting the makeshift cage into his arms and carrying it toward the bus stop. Although Minn had no idea what was happening, she did know one thing. She had to think fast. This was her chance.

◆

At the same time that Mitt was still trying to outrun Soren, a large bird swooped down, grasping Mitt in its bill and heading upward. Mitt had no idea what sort of bird it was as it all happened so fast. When he got his bearings about him, he saw it was a greater sandhill crane. It was an old crane, yet it seemed strong and willing.

Mitt found something familiar in the crane's face.

"I'm Trula. I'm Tuuli's sister," the crane told Mitt, in the way that cranes will tell such things.

"Long ago, your friend Tuuli asked me to keep watch over you and I have. It seemed you have been doing well taking care of yourself—that is, until now."

Trula swooned to Mitt, telling him that life often does not flow the way we want it to. She then added, looking downward at the beautiful river, "Do not push the river, it will flow by itself."

Mitt thought about that for a moment. He thought about Tuuli and her gentle spirit. He thought about all the other friends he had made on this journey so far. He

thought about Minn and the deep loss he was feeling now that she was gone for good. In the small quiet way that mice understand such ideas, Mitt understood what Trula was saying.

Trula didn't have to speak any further. Neither did Mitt. There, in the silence of the sky as autumn was pushing in against them, Trula winged northward. She was off her course and flying against what nature was telling her to do in order to honor a promise to her sister. Trula was watching out for Mitt and, for her, it meant carrying the little mouse to the big city.

But neither of them knew that in a short time, everything would change.

CHAPTER SIXTEEN
City Mouse

Minn remained quiet in her cage while seated on the lap of the girl's father. They were in the doctor's waiting room now, and Minn knew if she was going to escape, she had better do it now.

Minn waited for the father to become distracted by a commotion in the waiting room. It was a busy place with two parakeets, one cat, three dogs, and a weasel. Minn sized up one of the holes in the cover of her cage and knew that, if she pulled herself tight, she could fit right through it and scramble out. She could see that she would need to race all the way through the waiting room and out of the building without being caught.

"Mr. Charles," a voice said from the desk at the front of the room, "did you fill out your paperwork?"

Mr. Charles stepped up to the desk to answer the nurse, leaving the cage on the waiting room table unattended. Now was Minn's chance.

Minn tucked herself as small as she could and squeezed through the hole. She plopped out onto the table and scurried beneath the couch where she spotted a hole in the wall that took her straight outside. Mr. Charles did not notice her escaping, but the other animals in the waiting room did. They began to make noise at the sight of a mouse running across the floor.

But Minn couldn't worry about that. She had to keep her mind on one thing—get out the door and into the city.

Minn was free. Minn was free at last.

WHIRRRRRR! ROOOOOSH! Cars and buses and trucks were whizzing by, one after the next. They were speeding so fast that Minn could hardly catch sight of them. The streets were filled with people and bikes and strollers and market stands. The buildings went upward into the sky farther than Minn could see and it seemed that everything was moving much faster than Minn had ever seen.

"Hey, you," a gruff voice said. "Hey, you, with the dumb look on your face."

Minn turned.

Four rats standing
there laughed. "We
say 'dumb' and she
looks! How's that for
new to the city?"

Minn did not think
they were being very
nice. At first,
she felt a

little afraid being lost without Mitt
to help her, but then her scared
feeling turned into an angry feeling
when she realized she was being
teased in such a mean way.

"I mean," one of the rats continued, "this looks like a country
mouse."

Minn began to walk away. She shouldered herself up to the long building that ran the length of the street and kept her nose to the ground, trying to get away from the rats. But even so, they followed. She turned the corner and began to run.

The rats began to run, too.

Before she knew it, Minn was racing along the sidewalk as fast as she could and then WHOMP! She dropped through an open manhole cover, right into a cold, dark hole in the middle of the walkway. When she looked up, she saw the rats peering down at her.

And they didn't look friendly.

CHAPTER SEVENTEEN

The Rats

Trula landed along the waterfront in downtown Chicago. There were picnic tables with plenty of bread and cracker crumbs below, enough for both Trula and Mitt to find a small meal.

Lake Michigan was beautiful, but Mitt could tell the city of Chicago was much different than the Mackinaw State Forest in Michigan, where he grew up.

Thinking about the forest made him think about his parents and how it now was more important than ever to find them, and to tell them about Minn.

Back at the manhole, the rats peered into the open hole, one-by-one dropping into the opening where Minn was cowering. One, two, three, and four. The rats stood right in front of Minn and looked her straight in the eyes.

"You must be new in town," the largest one said. "We can help you."

At the waterfront, Trula told Mitt it was time for her to leave as she needed to catch up with the rest of her group and continue her southward journey. Mitt appreciated all that Trula had done for him. Before she left, he looked at the river and told her, in the best way that he could, that he did understand about the river. "I will not push it," he said. "I will let it flow on its own."

Hearing that, Trula nodded and left Chicago.

Mitt was now alone. Once again, he was alone. All alone, with nowhere to go.

◆

Back in the manhole, Minn was not quite sure whether to believe the rats or not. And then it happened.

In an unsuspecting but genuine way, one of the rats made a gesture with his paw that was known as a motion of kindness. It was a simple thing and done in the way that rats and mice will do. From this, Minn knew that, although they may talk differ-

ently than her and may behave a bit differently than her, it didn't mean that they were unkind. So, there in the middle of a storm drain with hundreds of people walking overhead, Minn told the rats her story and accepted their help.

Mitt, on the other side of town and believing that Minn was no longer alive, began to race toward the buildings that lined the street. He knew he had to start asking about his parents. Where could they be? Where were they staying?

At the same time across town, the rats urged Minn to follow them to their home. Minn scurried through tunnels and pipelines, across walkways and streets, often narrowly escaping the cars and motorcycles and buses.

When they arrived at the Navy Pier, it was almost bedtime and Minn was ready for sleep. The rats brought her into an abandoned garbage pail near the edge of the park area and, once inside, Minn fell fast asleep. The rats fell asleep, too, knowing that in the morning they would help Minn find her parents.

◆

That night Mitt found shelter near the entrance of a museum in the heart of the city. There were steps and a stoop in front, and Mitt found a crack right between the third and fourth stairs. It was growing colder at night now that it was early autumn, and Mitt was glad to have found a safe place to rest and stay warm.

As he drifted into sleep, his mind played with thoughts of Minn, and the sadness he felt over losing her overcame him. There in the middle of the big city with all its noise and hustle and bustle, Mitt wept small mouse-like tears, quietly and to himself, until he fell asleep.

◆

On the other side of the city, thinking that Mitt was gone for good, Minn did the same, in the darkness of a garbage pail, surrounded by creatures she did not know but had no choice but to trust.

CHAPTER EIGHTEEN

Navy Pier

In the morning the rats woke Minn and offered her doughnut crumbs and orange peels for breakfast. Minn was hungry enough to eat every last bite, but did not want to seem greedy to her new friends.

While eating, Minn asked, "Where do you

think my parents would be? Can you help me now? Have you met two white-footed mice recently?"

The rats had an idea.

"So this is how it will go," said the largest of the rats. "We will leave and make our way to the street near the Sears Tower. We have friends there, other rats like us, and we will ask them if they have seen any white-footed mice. We will tell them that if they have, they must tell us." Then the big one looked at Minn, his face serious. "You must not leave our home as there is much danger out there. We know the city."

With that Minn looked at the two rats who were assigned to remain in the pail with her. They nodded and let her know, in the hard but well intended way that rats will do, that they would make certain that she was safe ... for a while.

CHAPTER NINETEEN

Marny

That morning, Mitt went nose-first out of
the crack trying to avoid being seen. He
jumped into a nearby bush and began to
kick up the dirt looking for seed and
crumbs. He found the city a nice place to
be. It seemed most people were in such a
hurry they didn't notice a mouse wander-
ing about. There was much food and
plenty of places to find water.

Right then, a crowd of people came up to the door of the museum. It seemed as if they were waiting for the door to open, but they were blocking the entrance to his hideaway. All of a sudden Mitt noticed an osprey circling above. The bush offered little cover, and the people were still blocking his entrance into the hole. Right then, as the bird began to swoop down upon Mitt, the crowd began to file through the open door into the museum. Mitt had only one way to avoid the large bird and that was to move with the crowd of people.

◆

Meanwhile at the Navy Pier, Minn was growing restless. After such a large feast, the two rats fell asleep and Minn, thinking that perhaps she should begin to look for her parents, left the garbage pail and scurried right into the park.

There were crowds everywhere and more food than she had ever seen before. It was not the same sort of food that she found in the forest, or the same type of food that Gerdie made especially for her, but it was food all the same. There were leftover hot-dog buns, scattered potato chips, sweet sticks of half-eaten caramel apples, and her favorite, sticky pieces of crisp bread with sugar on top. Minn didn't have to work too hard to stay out of sight, either, as most people didn't seem to notice her and there were plenty of places to hide.

Then, Minn noticed something she had not seen before. To her left was a male red-winged blackbird, flitting back and forth in a nervous manner. Minn knew, much in the way that mice know such things, that this sort of bird was no danger to her, but what followed the red-winged blackbird most certainly was.

And now it was coming for Minn.

Minn tried to dart away from the ring-billed gull as it swooped in on her, but it was too late. Before she knew it, the gull had her firmly in its grasp and was heading skyward over the Navy Pier. The gull was Marny, and she quickly began swerving around food stands and above the carousel until three red-winged blackbirds began to chase them. Minn squirmed in the gull's bill, but Marny had no intention of dropping the mouse. And the blackbirds, who

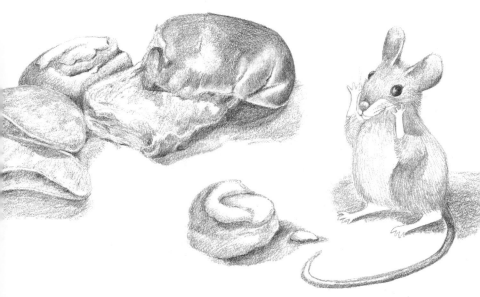

had been angered by how close Marny had been to their territory near the Ferris wheel, were not about to stop, either.

Both ways, it was no good for Minn.

CHAPTER TWENTY

The Museum

By now, Mitt was deep inside the Field
Museum of Natural History, hiding in a
scene set for woodland creatures such as
himself. There were two striped chip-
munks and an opossum, three cottontail
rabbits, and one white-tailed deer. Of

course, they were not alive, but they were made to look as if they were. Convinced this would be a safe place to hide, Mitt found a false log that looked very real and crawled inside to wait until dark. He had nowhere to go, no way to find his parents. What he needed now was sleep and time to think.

But that wasn't going to happen.

A group of school children had just entered the museum and their teacher was opening the door to the exhibit where Mitt was hiding. They were beginning to poke around and gently touch some of the items inside and, before Mitt knew it, one little boy found Mitt. Believing the mouse was part of the exhibit, he began patting Mitt on the head.

Mitt stood still. The little boy patted Mitt again, only this time a bit harder.

Mitt stood even more still. He did not blink. The little boy began to poke and needle Mitt a bit harder than he should have been doing. The teacher kept telling the young boy not to touch the mouse but the little boy did not listen.

The next moment, the little boy lifted his fist high into the air, intending to come down right upon Mitt's head. By now, Mitt had enough. The teacher's back was now turned, so Mitt had only one choice. He jumped up and landed on top of the little boy's head. Mitt then hopped down and raced out the open door and down the street as fast as he could.

◆

Meanwhile at the pier, the red-winged blackbirds were in fast pursuit of Marny and Minn. The gull was quickly confused

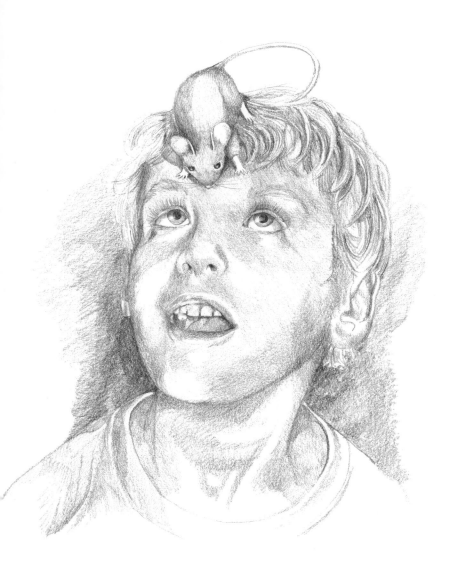

by the sights and sounds of the cars and
people and began to fly inward toward the
city. She dashed between rows of apart-
ment buildings and stores and flew over

telephone wires and through alleys and parking lots. All the while, the blackbirds were right behind her.

But when the red-winged blackbirds felt they were too far away from their territory and had chased the gull far enough, they turned around and headed back to the pier. However, Minn didn't have a moment to let out a sigh of relief because now Marny the gull was landing on a strip of lawn outside a row of large, old-fashioned houses with long porches. The gull placed one foot on Minn's belly.

It was almost over.

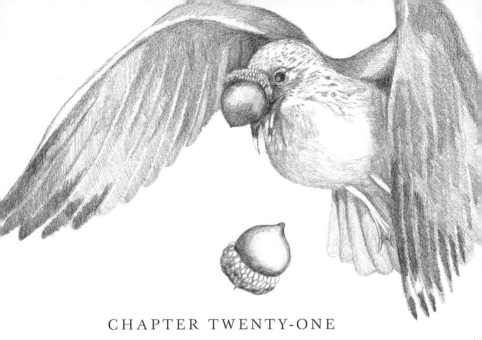

CHAPTER TWENTY-ONE

Acorns

Mitt, who was still rushing as far away from the museum as possible, didn't notice how he had ran all the way through the downtown and into a pretty street of well-kept houses. Each one was large and brightly painted. Mitt stopped to catch his breath.

That's when he heard a squeal.

Mitt knew in an instant, in the way that mice know the familiar sounds of other mice, that the squeal belonged to Minn. When he saw the gull lowering its head and opening its bill, Mitt did the only thing he could think of doing.

The boulevard was lined with trees of all sorts, linden trees and white mulberry, silver maple and serviceberry trees. But Mitt saw a giant white oak tree not far from the gull and, beneath it, were fallen acorns. Mitt stood behind the tree and One! Two! Three! He began to toss acorns at the gull's head.

Plop! Plop! Plop!

The moment the gull looked up, Wham! Mitt tossed a huge acorn right between its eyes. The commotion had disturbed a kestrel from its roost and, as the kestrel dived down, the gull flew away. Mitt raced to Minn's side, almost in disbelief that it was truly her lying there on the grass.

Minn, too, thought perhaps she was dreaming when she saw Mitt. But there was no time to talk about what had happened as the pair had no choice but to scramble for safety from the kestrel coming down for them both.

The pair spotted a middle-aged man on the porch with a broom, the door to his home open wide. They ran in without notice. The man did see the kestrel, and he raised his broom to it. Inside, Mitt and Minn did a silent cheer. As much as they were cheering that the kestrel, the gull, and the blackbirds were gone, they were cheering to be together again.

The house was very large. There were four beautiful velvet couches in the parlor and copper lamps on every table. There was a

fireplace with a carved mantel, old clocks, and pictures in frames everywhere.

Mitt and Minn didn't want to waste too much time talking about why they were separated and where they had been. Time was running out. The last leaf of autumn had fallen and, if they were to find their parents, they had better do it soon. Before Mitt and Minn had a chance to find a quiet corner for their home, the middle-aged man walked into the room and shut the door.

He spotted the mice. And he was holding a broom.

CHAPTER TWENTY-TWO
Richard

"Well, hello there, you little darlings," he said. Mitt and Minn both understood the man, much in the way that mice can understand smiling men, and so they didn't back away when he came closer.

The pair was sitting on a library table next to an old dusty dictionary. Mitt began to sneeze.

The man laughed. He held out his hand and said, "I will find a better place for you than this!"

With that, the man took Mitt and Minn to an old dollhouse set up on a table in the middle of the sunroom. The sunroom was painted bright yellow, and there were blue-and-white curtains on all nine windows. The dollhouse was very large and had many rooms with soft beds just the right size for Mitt and Minn.

The man placed Mitt upon the tiny red couch in the dollhouse living room, while he put Minn upon a bed in the master bedroom. Once he had settled them there, the man gave another laugh and said, "I always hoped this antique would come in handy for something; feels really nice to put it to use!"

Mitt and Minn felt at ease in his home, and let him know, in the best way they could, that they knew he was kind and that they were not afraid of him.

"I'm Richard," the man said. "I own this bed and breakfast. You may stay here as long as you like."

With that, Richard walked away, only to return moments later with a small plate of dried cherries, bits of Swiss cheese, and one large slice of oatmeal bread. Minn was so excited to eat that she knocked over a stack of thread spools displayed on the table outside the dollhouse.

"Truth is," he said, "I don't get much in the way of business here anymore, and I could really use the company. The only company I seem to have is that ghost. She just won't leave."

Mitt and Minn swallowed very slowly. For a brief while it seemed they were living in the best place two road-weary mice could live. But a ghost?

Richard must have seen the worry on their faces. "Oh, but it's a nice ghost, I know that much. When there are crumbs on the table, the crumbs vanish overnight. If I lose something, it's right where it should be the next day. This is a very helpful ghost, and a nice one, at that."

And then his face turned sad. "It's just that ever since people started talking about my bed-and-breakfast having a ghost, I don't get as many visitors. Truth is, I'm getting sort of lonesome."

Mitt and Minn felt sorry as they listened to Richard's story. It must be sad to have such a lovely business as his and not have customers—all because of a ghost that won't leave. But even so, Mitt and Minn weren't exactly sure they wanted to meet this ghost.

When Richard said goodnight and turned out the lights, Mitt and Minn fell into a very deep sleep. In the morning, the first

thing Mitt noticed was that the plate Richard had used to serve them bread and cheese was completely clean. The spools of thread Minn had knocked over earlier were neatly stacked just as they had been the day before.

"Mitt," asked Minn, "did you do that?"

"No," whispered Mitt. "Didn't you?"

Right then Richard appeared with a cup of morning coffee for himself and a saucer of cream for Mitt and Minn. "See," he said, "I told you so."

It was true. The house was haunted.

CHAPTER TWENTY-THREE

Gerdie

Later that day, Mitt and Minn told Richard their story. They told him how they had come very far to find their parents, and how it seemed as if they never would.

Richard understood the mice. "It is almost winter now, and far too dangerous for you to be trying to find your parents. You must stay where it is warm and safe. They are probably doing the same thing." Then Richard had an idea. "Stay with me through the winter, and I will help you find your parents in the spring."

It seemed like a good idea to Mitt and Minn, who enjoyed Richard's company very much. He kept them warm and well fed, and told them stories all day long. There was something familiar in his smile, something Minn couldn't quite explain.

Minn wasn't quite sure it was a good idea to stay all winter, but Mitt told her about Trula and how Trula told him not to push the river, it will flow by itself. Minn thought about that and agreed. "But I'm afraid of the ghost," said Minn to Mitt. "I'm not sure I like living in a house with a ghost!"

As each day came closer to full winter, each night the ghost did something more and more unusual. And each night, Mitt and Minn tried very hard to stay out of its way.

One cold snowing night before bedtime, Richard made a fire in the fireplace, and he set Mitt and Minn on top of the mantel so they would get good and warm from the heat before bed.

And that's when it happened.

Mitt and Minn sat quietly in between dozens of photographs, each one in a different frame—some small and ornate with delicate decoration around the border, some large and wooden and very old.

It was there that Minn spotted a familiar face in a photograph. She went closer to see the woman. She was young and looked lovely. Richard stood up from stoking the fire and said to Minn, "That's my mother. I haven't seen her in a very long time and it makes me sad."

And that's when Minn knew. The woman in the picture was Gerdie long ago. Gerdie was Richard's mother!

Minn did not know how to tell Richard that she knew his mother and that his mother had been a

mother to her, too. Although she was good at sending messages in the subtle ways that mice can do, this was too much of a story for her to tell him in a simple way.

That night, when Minn went to bed, she fell asleep thinking about how sad Gerdie was when the locket given to her by her son was broken, and how much Gerdie wanted to see her son once more. Although Minn never knew what happened between them, she did know that both of them were sad inside and wanted to be together somehow.

Right before drifting off to sleep, Minn told Mitt that, in the morning, she would figure out a way to let Richard know about Gerdie.

But that chance never arrived for Minn.

CHAPTER TWENTY-FOUR
The Ghost

In the middle of the night, there was a loud crashing sound in the parlor. Several of the photographs fell off the mantel, and then it sounded as if a vase was tipped over.

It was the ghost. And it sounded angry.

"Oh, no," whispered Mitt to Minn. "What do we do?"

There was one last flicker of light from an ember in the fireplace, casting a glow all

throughout the parlor. It wasn't bright, but it was just enough so that Mitt and Minn could see, whether they wanted to or not.

"We must wake Richard," said Mitt. The pair crept out into the living room, hoping to run up the stairs to Richard's room.

CRASH! The dictionary on the library table fell on the floor, causing all sorts of other books near it to fall off the table.

Mitt and Minn were in the middle of the room when, all of a sudden, they were face-to-face with the ghost.

The pair shrieked. The ghost shrieked. All they saw of each other in the dimly lit room were subtle outlines of shadows against the walls. They all continued shrieking until their eyes adjusted.

It wasn't a ghost! It was another white-footed

mouse. No, it was a pair of white-footed mice!

And in an instant, Mitt and Minn knew exactly who they were.

There, in the middle of the room with only a bit of firelight to grace them, Mitt and Minn recognized their parents. Each of them knew, in the ways that mice know, that they were family and from now on they would always be together.

As they nuzzled, Mitt and Minn's mother told them how, when they had arrived in Chicago, they went to the bus stop and hid in a traveler's suitcase. They came to the bed-and-breakfast with the traveler, hoping to stay out of sight while they thought of a way to get back to Michigan. When they first came to Richard's, it was a busy place with lots of visitors staying and having a good time.

And then their mother went on, "From the first night we arrived, I wanted to help keep the house tidy, so I pitched in here and there, cleaning up when I could and helping people find things whenever they misplaced them. But soon people stopped coming." And then, lowering her voice to a near hush so Richard wouldn't wake, she added, "And I have no idea why."

Mitt and Minn didn't know whether to laugh or cry. They had found their parents. There wasn't a ghost. But, quickly breaking their reunion, Mitt's father spoke up. "We must all get back to Michigan. We can't wait any longer. The boat's leaving."

Their father took them over to a newspaper sitting on an end table. They recognized a word and some letters, much in the way mice can recognize such details. They noted the letters that spelled MACKINAW, and saw a picture of a ship with Christmas trees upon it. There was a date of December 2 on the newspaper, and it matched the date on the calendar nearby.

All mice knew of this ship. Mitt was sure he had sailed on it before. After unloading the trees in Chicago for Christmas, the ship would return to Cheboygan. It was their only ride back. It was their only way home.

They had to leave now, or they wouldn't make it.

CHAPTER TWENTY-FIVE

Good-bye

"But wait!" cried Minn.

While preparing to leave, Minn told her parents about Gerdie and how Gerdie had taken care of her for such a very long time. At this, Minn's mother took on a soft look in her eyes, a feeling of instant love and thankfulness for the woman who had taken care of her baby mouse. Minn told how she discovered that Richard must be Gerdie's son, and how she couldn't leave without letting Richard know that his mother was very lonesome for him.

Minn's parents listened to her story. And then Minn's mother, wise in the ways of a mother's heart, had an idea.

In the stack of books that had fallen on the floor was a book of phone numbers and addresses. Together the mice lifted the pages until the letter "M," and it was there. It said Mom. 555-432-7093. They left the book open where Richard would be sure find it.

"Trust me," said Minn's mother. "When he sees the book, he will know what to do."

The mice were making a bit of noise as they were scuttling to get out of the house, and it woke Richard. He came down the stairs and saw the mess. Curious, he began to look around. Although Mitt and Minn wanted to say good-bye to Richard right then, the four mice knew they had no time to do so. They must leave through the front door at that very moment or they would never make it to the ship *Mackinaw* in time.

But, in the quiet of night, as they were all slipping through the crack in the front door, Minn took one last look behind her. In the faint glow of the last ember, she saw Richard's shadow against the wall. He was holding the address book in one hand, and the phone in the other. Minn knew it was all right to leave.

CHAPTER TWENTY-SIX

Mackinaw

The foursome exchanged stories and tales on the way down to the waterfront. They moved very fast and made certain not to lose sight of each other. They all were trembling with excitement but yet disbelief that, after all they had been through, they were finally together.

When they reached the waterfront, the boat was there, and the trees had already

been unloaded, except for a few that would remain for the ride back to Michigan. The four skittered across the icy dock and each had to leap onto the boat's edge.

First Mitt. Then his mother and father. Next came Minn. One, two, three— SPLASH! Minn didn't make it. Three were on the boat but Minn was struggling in the water below—and the boat was starting to pull away.

Mitt wasn't about to lose his sister again. He remembered what Abe Lincoln had said. A house divided will not stand. All at once, Mitt jumped into the icy water to save Minn.

At the same time, the anchor was being lifted. Mitt saw it right away and he directed Minn to hang on. There, in the middle of the nearly frozen water, Mitt and Minn held onto the anchor as it was pulled upward toward the boat. And, for the first time in a long time, there was something else there to warm them when they needed it—their parents.

The four huddled in a life vest set near the boiler room on the boat, gathering whatever heat they could. Once they regained their footings, their father spoke up.

"It's been a long journey for all of us. I'm so happy that we are together again the way it should be for a family of white-footed mice. Now, the minute we reach shore, we have one more thing to do."

Mitt and Minn were listening. "What?" asked Mitt.

Mitt's parents spoke at the same time.

"We have to find the others!"

◆

And that's how it came to be that a family of four white-footed mice came riding home to Michigan one winter afternoon.

They arrived in Cheboygan on a boat, right back where they had started. Now that they had found each other again, new adventures were waiting. And as Mitt and Minn had learned on that icy cold night in Lake Michigan, they had more brothers and sisters than they ever knew, each one scattered to a different place because of a mishap that happened a long time ago.

And Mitt and Minn would find them someday, too, because although Mitt never did find his mitten and Minn never was able to return to Ely, they had found something more important along the way, and that was—to a willing heart, nothing is impossible.

The End

IN 2006, MITTEN PRESS started a series of chapter books about a lively pair of white-footed mice named Mitt and Minn. In each book, readers are sure to learn more than a little about a Midwestern state as they travel along with the mice. We hope you've had a chance to read them all:

Book One: *Mitt, the Michigan Mouse*
ISBN: 978-1-58726-303-3

Book Two: *Minn from Minnesota*
ISBN: 978-1-58726-304-0

Book Three: *Mitt & Minn at the Wisconsin Cheese Jamboree*
ISBN: 978-1-58726-305-7

Book Four: *Mitt & Minn's Illinois Adventure*
ISBN: 978-1-58726-306-4

Join Mitt & Minn's Midwest Readers by sending your email address to the publisher at ljohnson@mittenpress.com. You will receive updates on future series by Mitten Press and fun activities to go along with the books to challenge what you know about the Midwest states.

www.mittenpress.com

So Long Jamboree!
WISCONSIN
CHICAGO
IOWA
Nelson Farm
Moline
Schwindle Brothers
FEED
FEED
Illinois River
ILLINOIS
INDIANA
MISSISSIPPI River
QUINCY
MARK TWAIN NAT. WILDLIFE REFUGE COMPLEX HEADQUARTERS
SPRINGFIELD
Lake Springfield
MARK TWAIN NAT. WILDLIFE REFUGE (Two Rivers NWR Headquarters
Alton
MISSOURI
Rend Lake
MINN
Mitt
SHAWNEE NATIONAL FOREST
KENTUCKY